Finding Waihona

Book Two of the Singular Cat Series

By

Vicki Spandel

Illustrated by
Jeni Kelleher

Written by Vicki Spandel
Illustrated by Jeni Kelleher
Illustrations Prepared for Print by Dennis Schmidling, Sisters Gallery
Layout and Design by Steve Peha

Vicki's photo courtesy of Lynn Woodward, woodwardcreative.com

Printed in the United States of America.

Published by Singular Books
An imprint of Platform Publishing

Steve Peha
543 NE 84th Street
Seattle, WA 98115
stevepeha@gmail.com

ISBN: 978-0-9972831-5-0

Table of Contents

Dedicated to my beloved friend,
Darle Fearl, gifted teacher and reader.
Your voice lives in my heart.

And above all, watch with glittering
eyes the whole world around you
because the greatest secrets are
always hidden in the most unlikely
places. Those who don't believe in
magic will never find it.

~ Roald Dahl, The Minpins

Introduction

When I was small, my favorite book was *Winnie the Pooh*. I loved Ernest H. Shepard's map of "The 100 Aker Wood," showing where Pooh, Piglet, Eeyore, and A. A. Milne's other endearing characters lived. We look down on the place "where the woozle wasn't," a spot that's "nice for piknicks," Pooh's "trap for the heffalumps," and other sites that made up Winnie's world.

Milne knew he had to let his gentle bear roam freely to share his kindness with others. So, he created a whole village, where Winnie and the reader could wander together.

After *No Ordinary Cat* (Book 1 of this series) was published, many people asked about a sequel. I loved the idea, but knew it would only work if I gave Rufus his own "100 Aker Wood." Space to explore—sometimes safely, often not—encountering characters he couldn't meet in Mr. Peabody's back yard.

As *Finding Waihona* opens, Rufus feels compelled to reunite with Asha, the feral friend he's not seen in weeks. Doing so, however, means venturing into a far bigger world, one both irresistible and terrifying. Running for his life one day, Rufus discovers… Waihona.

Waihona is a Hawaiian word for a place to store things. Books, for example. *Hale waihona puke* is Hawaiian for a building that stores books: the library.

In this story, Waihona is a hidden lookout where Rufus and Asha seek refuge from a coyote on the hunt. For two human characters, Jack and Lexi, that lookout becomes a sanctuary, an other-worldly retreat where they escape everyday life to share innermost feelings and dreams.

If you think this word feels magical, you're right—but here's the truly magical part.

Most things we treasure are either non-material or too big to hold in our hands: friendship, love, the land, family, freedom, and more. Such things cannot be stored in a treasure chest—or even a mystical tree fort. We keep them in our minds and hearts. And because we do, waihona, that place where we safeguard what we hold sacred, takes on a new and deeper meaning.

For the characters in this story, finding waihona requires first figuring out what they treasure most. Some are wise enough to know, while others are still working it out. For them, as for us, *Finding Waihona* is a journey into the soul.

Prologue

Many couples meet through a mutual friend. Only a select few can boast their matchmaker was a cat. For R. J. Peabody the poet and Lin RuShi, gardener, singer, and baker extraordinaire, it came about this way.

Rufus, the matchmaker in question, lived with Mrs. Lin for most of his first year on earth, then ventured into the wilderness one day on a whim—and was nearly drowned by an ill-tempered goose.

Now, the odds of a poet happening along when one is drowning are extremely low, but Rufus had the sort of luck most cats would kill for.

After being rescued by Mr. Peabody, who'd never given much thought to cats before, Rufus couldn't very well trot on home as

if nothing had happened. The poet had saved his life. And was a phenomenal cook to boot. It seemed only fitting to linger for... well, however long it might take to show boundless appreciation.

As the days ticked by, Rufus grew increasingly fond of this gentle man, who spared no pains to make his guest feel at home. If there was a heaven for cats, Rufus was certain they served crab cakes there. And provided feather beds like the one Mr. Peabody had made just for him. And didn't allow geese.

Rufus assumed the gardener would show up when she got round to it. But knowing nothing of Rufus's whereabouts made that difficult. RuShi was, in fact, searching everywhere a human might imagine a cat going. Which admittedly isn't everywhere they go.

It's said, logically enough, that we find things in the last place we look—and that's where the gardener found her dear Rufus: by a cozy woodstove, safe and well-fed, having developed a lifelong passion for crab cakes. And surprisingly, for books.

Once things got sorted out, poet and gardener might have gone their separate ways—and indeed, they tried that for a time, but being apart left them longing to share things both treasured. Tea and scones. Poetry by moonlight. Laughter. Music. The love of a cat. And eventually, each other.

They wed on a sun-kissed morning in early spring, amidst lavish displays of iris and greenery assembled and ribboned by the bride. Delighted guests took home every frond and flower at the end of this glorious day. Along with wedges of lemon and raspberry cake, also courtesy of the bride. No one had dressed up, including the newlyweds. Everyone agreed it was the best wedding ever.

Their decision to live in R. J.'s house made sense. It was near the ocean both loved, and offered RuShi ample space for growing this and that. Still, saying goodbye to her little cabin was hard. From her rocker right down to her baking utensils and beloved garden boots, everything held memories that clung to her like old friends. Emptying the cabin felt like emptying her soul.

When the last keepsake was packed, RuShi stood in the doorway, staring at the cold fireplace and recalling how once, right there, she'd sung her heart out, rocking a tiny, homesick kitten to sleep.

Outside the window, iris waved farewell from the garden she and Rufus had planted together. RuShi smiled, recalling the small cat pouncing on each spot where a tender new plant should be given a chance at life. *I won't forget you,* she whispered. To the garden. The cabin. The memories.

That night, the couple sat together in the home they now shared, planning ways to fill summer days that always seem endless when viewed from spring. They'd plant a thousand flowers, create volumes of poems and recipes, conquer sourdough, walk barefoot on pristine beaches that stretched to the sun. For once, they let themselves dream without limits. Thank heavens. Limits ruin everything.

Rufus, snuggled between them, was making plans of his own—of which the newlyweds were blissfully unaware. That was just as well. If humans knew half the things cats get up to, they'd never sleep.

CHAPTER ONE

You're Gonna Love It Here!

When Jack and his mom Sam first entered RuShi's former cabin, it was deserted as a house can get. Their footsteps echoed off the wooden floors, and kitchen drawers hung open like so many tongues sticking out. Before them rose a daunting mountain of moving boxes stuffed with bits and pieces of their former life.

"I remembered it bigger," Sam said. Was she referring to the house? Or the cardboard mountain?

Jack didn't know. And didn't care. He had other worries. Would kids in his new school tease him? *Hey, Red—is that hair of yours on fire? Or did you paint it that color on purpose?* Sidesplitting.

Someone had told him red hair symbolized courage. If so, why didn't he feel more like Braveheart?

15

"Don't worry," Sam was saying. "We'll turn this place into home." *Unlikely*, Jack thought. How could anywhere be home when someone you loved could never, ever be there?

Jack reached for a box he was pretty sure held baseball gear. It didn't. By sheer rotten chance, the first thing he unwrapped was a photo he couldn't bear to look at. His dad holding up a glove, awaiting the pitch. Jack could still hear the beautiful *whap* of a baseball hitting leather.

Keep that arm in shape till I get back had been Sgt. Cody Rooker's last words to his son—right before the helicopter crash. A "technical failure" the report called it. *Technically*, Jack thought, *the end of my world.*

"You'll see," Sam said, stacking more dishes than Jack thought any reasonable person could use in a lifetime, "You're gonna love it here."

16

Sam's persistent cheeriness was driving Jack bonkers. He didn't "love it here" yet, that's for sure, and smiling nonstop was more exhausting than running a marathon.

"Wanna look outside while I finish the kitchen?" Sam asked, and Jack jumped at the chance—literally. Anything was better than digging through more family history.

The back door opened into paradise. Iris and lilies by the hundreds spilled into a primeval forest alive with birds. A creek threaded its way through swaths of lime and forest green moss, and giant ferns rose up like something out of Jurassic Park.

From beneath those ferns, emerald eyes followed Jack's every move.

2

CHAPTER TWO

You Could Do Worse

Rufus had known from the start that his two favorite humans belonged together, though they'd been a bit slow to pick up on the obvious. With gardener and poet under one roof, Rufus no longer needed to make that dangerous house-to-house trek, dodging bloodthirsty carnivores. He made it anyway.

Even without RuShi's cheery presence, the cabin where Rufus had grown up called to him. He'd lie near the creek for hours, immersed in the harmonies of redwings, frogs, and katydids.

Today, a newcomer was stretched out right in the big cat's favorite spot. Emerging from the ferns, Rufus climbed onto the intruder's chest, trilling softly. Whether Jack was more startled or elated is hard to say. He sat up and began stroking Rufus with that easygoing touch cats trust.

"You must've read my mind," Jack said, feeling an instant bond with this red-haired creature. "I could use a friend about now." At last. Someone Jack could open up to without weighing every word.

"I miss my dad so much it hurts," he began. "Mom puts on happiness like a costume—when I know she's broken inside. If she says 'You're gonna love it here' one more time, I think I'll explode."

When you need to tell someone your troubles, you could do worse than a cat. They know instinctively that the eyes and heart reveal more than words. Unlike humans, cats offer comfort without attaching a lot of unwanted, pesky advice. And when it comes to keeping a secret, they are what the French might call *sans pareil*.

"I wish you lived right here," Jack said. The funny part was, Rufus *did* live there—sort of. Just not all the time.

Jack's mom was calling, so the boy stood. "You're the best listener ever," he told the cat. "If only you liked unpacking boxes."

20

Actually, there is almost nothing cats enjoy more, though some might consider their technique a bit slapdash.

Humans were restless beings, Rufus thought. When they were in, they wanted out. Once out, they were itching to go in. Apparently, Jack was staying put for now. So, Rufus started down the trail to the Peabodys' house, weaving through shimmery grasses, keeping an eye out for testy Canada geese, who found it humorous to nest where others liked to walk.

CHAPTER THREE

Savage Alien

Rufus meant to visit the cabin the following morning, but awoke consumed by one thought: finding Asha. He missed his soulmate the way winter-weary trees miss sunshine.

Asha's year-old kit, Razi, guided Rufus to the blackberry tunnel beyond the Peabodys' back fence. Dark. Thorny. The route the black cat had taken when leaving the poet's house to resume her life in the wild. Long and serpentine, it led to the ocean inlet Asha loved. She had to be there.

"It's safer than it looks," Razi was saying. "Hawks can't dive through thistles. It's too small for raccoons, and the snakes are harmless enough, even if some don't know it. The one thing you might need to worry about is… well, never mind. Perhaps I should go with you."

Rufus wasn't listening. He was eyeing the opening, calculating whether he'd fit. A prickly tunnel would be one miserable place to get stuck.

Had he remembered to tell Razi everything? Though they lived under the same roof, the kit with a feral mother found the human brain a knotty puzzle—and would need all his wits to keep the household running smoothly until the red cat returned.

"Humans are sensitive," Rufus reminded the young cat. For the third time. "Listen when the poet speaks—even if you can make no sense of it. The gardener's a hugger. Just go along. Whatever you do, don't chase birds. Or butterflies. That upsets her."

Razi rolled his eyes. "Holy huckleberries! Got it! But hurry back. Being you wears me to rubble."

The passage was indeed snug for a well-rounded cat, and blackberry brambles plucked at Rufus's fur the whole way. He stepped out into fog so thick he couldn't see his own feet—yet, through the swirls, he glimpsed something ominous coming his way. A monstrous head sprouting... what? Tiny trees?

24

The head was perched on ridiculously long, spindly legs. Who required legs like that? Some grotesque cat-eating spider? With those feather duster ears, one could, Rufus thought, hear anything. Caterpillars munching. Ants marching.

He shrank into his smallest self, which, thanks to numerous crab cakes, felt nowhere near small enough. Then, *oh mercy...* their noses touched. *Help*, he tried to say, but nothing came out, and there was no one to rescue him anyway. He'd seen to that, hadn't he? *Would this be the grisly end to his search for Asha? How long would it take this spidery thing to eat a modestly large cat?* Rufus couldn't bear to look.

When at last he opened his eyes, he was still whole, the fog had parted, and the creature was gone. Relief washed over him. He'd come nose to nose with a savage alien. And survived.

Through the pines he spied an L-shaped dock, and at its angle stood a man waving something over his head. Humans meant food, and stressful situations always left Rufus famished.

26

Then he saw it. A dog. Its coppery coat thick and lustrous, its dark eyes watchful. The beast rose to his full height, well above the man's knees, waiting for Rufus to make the first move.

Even the tiniest dog spelled trouble. This one looked big enough to swallow him whole. Still, he'd stood up to that nosy behemoth with grassy breath. Was he going to let a dog put the kibosh on this mission? As he pondered that, Asha appeared out of nowhere, strutting along the dock as if she owned it.

"Right on time there, rat patrol!" the man said with a laugh, tossing Asha a fish she was clearly expecting. She slipped from sight, never drawing a glance from the dog. What was up with that?

Suddenly, it dawned on Rufus. This weather-beaten dock was the feral cat's renowned hideaway. She dwelt here—for the time being—smack under the big dog's feet.

In fact, Asha had reclaimed her old lodgings a few weeks back, evicting a snaggle-toothed thief no one missed much. And making one fisherman very happy.

CHAPTER FOUR

No Match for This Cat

Rainy Day Doolittle they called him. He fished in all weathers, and oh my, how that man could make a line sing. "When the sun goes into hiding, the fish come out to play," he'd say with a wink, as if this bit of wisdom were so obvious that everyone ought to be netting the big ones.

Rainy had caught more than his share. He was lucky that way, people said. But Rainy didn't believe in luck when it came to fishing. "Gotta be smarter than the fish," was how he put it. "And that I am." Outwitting a kleptomaniac, however, would take specialized expertise.

For months, the fisherman had been pestered by a no-good rodent holed up beneath the dock. The scalawag crept in whenever the big dog wasn't looking, snatching anything in Rainy's creel.

Then one morning, the scruffy bandit stopped showing up, and Rainy figured he'd keeled over in a pile of clam shells somewhere. Or tangled with a crab too ornery for him. But when he spotted the cat, he knew. That little tiger could vanquish the most arrogant rodent. What Rainy did not know was that the cat had been watching him too. For days.

Asha had never been drawn to humans. But this one had a toy she found irresistible. It consisted of a pole with a thin line fastened to it, and at the end of that line was an insect-like thingamabob made of feathers and whatnot. The man played with it endlessly, swinging the pole back, pausing for a split second, then slinging it forward till that little gizmo hit the water. This was entertainment made for a cat. And it got better.

The toy attracted fish. Lots of fish. Once they went after it, they couldn't let go. The man brought in so many that surely, she thought, he could spare one for her. But then... there was the dog. Big as a bear, with feet the size of Asha's head.

To top it off, a cat could grow old and rickety waiting for that goliath to leave the man's side. That was the trouble with dogs. They'd hang around humans for hours. Annoying.

Finally, the time felt right. It was pre-dawn, misting silver, and the dog was lost in a dream. Asha heard the familiar whirrrrrr of the line rolling out—and saw it go taut.

Silent as shade, she stole down the dock, eyes darting from Rainy to the dog and back. She got within inches before Rainy reeled in a pocket-sized catch. "Nice try, pipsqueak," he told the rockfish. "Come back when you're dinner." His voice roused the dog, who unveiled one enormous eye.

Fish in hand, Rainy turned to see Asha standing her ground, daring Mac to try something.

"It's you," he said. "The feisty scrapper who dispatched that hooligan rat. Here for the reward?" Rainy arced the fish high, intending it to land far back from Mac. Asha didn't wait. She rose straight up, twisting midair to seize her prize, vaporizing into the mist.

31

"Did you see that?" the fisherman asked.

The big dog had seen, all right. A hornswoggling rat was nothing. Gravity itself was no match for this cat.

Not Your Everyday Dog

Rainy's best friend had walked into his life one day looking for a bite to eat and a friendly voice, and finding both, decided to stay. He'd been gaunt as kindling, but Rainy soon remedied that, sharing down to the last scrap with a dog who seemed forever hungry, but never made a fuss about it.

When someone turns up to sweep loneliness from your life, you can't call him by any old name. After much thought, Rainy settled on Mac in honor of a buddy who'd meant worlds to him in another time. The big dog took to it right off as if he'd been waiting for someone to figure out what his name was.

Mac's pedigree was a matter of speculation. He had a Lab's good nature—but enough bulk to make two of them. He may have had some Newfoundland in his ancestry, for he could out-swim any dog Rainy had ever seen, jumping from the dock for any

reason or no reason at all, circling the cove tirelessly. "If I'm ever 'bout to drown, Mac, feel free to float my way," Rainy would tell him. "You're a canine life raft."

They bunked in a cabin steps from the inlet. "A hike too short to cool your coffee," Rainy liked to say. He sold fish to nearby markets, restaurants, and locals, among whom he was something of a legend. His income from this endeavor was modest, but then, he had needs to match.

Mac had minimal interest in fish, but like friends everywhere, was happy to do whatever Rainy found amusing, even if he didn't quite get what all the excitement was about. The two got into a routine. Rising before dawn, making coffee, grabbing the pole and flies, and heading to the dock at first light. Though he'd never tasted it and likely never would, Mac loved the smell of coffee. It smelled of contentment and anticipation. Good times. Something about the steam rising from Rainy's thermos, mingling with mist from the bay, made Mac feel the world was rolling along the way it should.

Then one day the cat arrived on the scene. And things got a stitch more complicated.

Many a dog would have gone after that cat at the first chance. But Mac wasn't your everyday sort of dog. He'd grown up around cats, and had infinite respect for their cleverness. They could do things he couldn't. Sneak up on birds. Land on four feet from mind-blowing heights. Most remarkable of all, they could devour a whole fish and leave the skeleton intact. You had to admire that.

This cat could clearly take care of herself most of the time. Mac meant to be around for the other times. He'd mind his own business when she came round for fish, though that was one thing about cats he never would understand. Their bizarre food preferences. Just thinking about it was enough to bring on a sneezing fit.

CHAPTER SIX

Spellbound

Earth to Eeyore! Must you be so gloomy?"

Yes, Jack thought. *I must.* He knew his mom was trying to look on the so-called bright side, if there even was such a thing, but he wasn't ready to go all Mary Poppins yet.

It might have helped had their ideas of "fun" matched. Jack would have preferred washing a hundred windows to baking one more cookie. He suggested hunting for fossils. Maybe bringing home a snake.

When Sam failed to swoon over this heart-stopping opportunity, Jack scrounged up the baseball mitts. But mitt or not, Sam couldn't handle his fastballs. Did he have to throw so hard? *Hard?* She called that *hard?* If he could, Jack would level an oak or two.

Monopoly? Please. While Sam lit up like fireworks every time she landed on Boardwalk, Jack thought if you'd played one Monopoly game, you'd played them all.

At least they weren't chained in a dungeon. Jack had his own room, big enough for bunk beds, a desk, and a beanbag chair. So far, he had only the beanbag chair. But still. *Snap out of it,* he told himself. *You have the world's best mom—even if she doesn't catch fastballs. Or snakes.*

As the two slipped into their latest funk, someone knocked, and they nearly collided racing for the door. Jack swung it wide, and was instantly spellbound—by a girl with mesmerizing eyes, long hair blue-black as ravens' wings, and a shark tooth hanging from her neck. She smiled. "Got any milk?"

Please, God, let there be milk in that fridge, Jack thought.

"It's for Nina," Jack heard the girl say as they ushered her in. "She's a goat."

"A goat?" Sam asked, holding the fridge door open and "cooling the whole darn room," something she'd repeatedly asked Jack not to do.

"We're bottle feeding her," the visitor continued, watching Sam fill a tall pitcher. "A coyote got her mother. I'm Lexi, by the way—our farm's just over that hill."

Were her eyes changing color with the light?

"Let me carry that," Jack offered, reaching for the pitcher. "It would give me a chance to meet Nina." Sam had been telling him he needed to make new friends. She probably hadn't meant goats, but you had to start somewhere.

Those iridescent eyes turned to Jack. "Thank you—and don't worry. It's not far."

Jack wasn't worried. He could hike to the moon and back. He'd just landed on Boardwalk.

40

CHAPTER SEVEN

Beware of Shortcuts

Watch for weasels," Razi warned. "They hunt in the early hours, same as us."

Us? Rufus had never stalked so much as a grasshopper—early, late, or any time. Why would anyone pursue such an unsavory hobby with perfectly good food waiting in the kitchen? And—weasels? "Do they have legs like willow sprigs?" he asked. "And shrubbery erupting from their heads?"

"How do you come up with this poppycock?" Razi asked. "Listen. Take me along this time. I'll scare up a weasel or two so you'll know what to look for." His eyes glimmered at the prospect.

Scaring up things that might want to eat you sounded like an insane form of amusement—just the sort of thing Asha's kit

would go for. "You'd best protect the humans," the red cat quipped. "Weasels could be anywhere." *Were weasels even a real thing?*

Ducking into the tunnel, Rufus squeezed through the briars, inhaling the rich blackberry aroma. Near the end of the twisty labyrinth, chickadees and nuthatches flitted madly, raising a cacophony of chatter that Razi—had he been allowed on this trip— would have recognized as a warning.

Unexpected as a hiccup, a short-legged menace planted itself at the exit, trapping Rufus. It had the face of a miniature fox, and the disturbing look of a creature to whom fear is a total stranger. Sinister eyes drilled into the red cat with unblinking ferocity. *It's hypnotizing me,* Rufus realized.

A black streak shot past, and like that, the beady-eyed hypnotist was gone.

"I take it that was your first weasel," said a clump of brush— parting to reveal Asha. "Dodgy imps," she added. "Never look one in the eye. They can barely kill things fast enough to keep up with

their appetites." This was a fine hello after weeks apart. More weasel tips. Unaccompanied by any gushy glad-to-see-you's.

Asha was already edging through the grove, and the heady blend of fish, pine, and salt air pulled Rufus after her. Sandy earth cushioned his feet with every step. Terns and gulls cried out, diving through glassy waves for fingerlings. Then… there it was. The horrific brute who'd forced Rufus into retreat a few days before. "I had no idea dogs came that big," he whispered.

"Big isn't everything," Asha said. *It is if you're small*, Rufus thought.

He watched Asha traipse nonchalantly toward the dock. Having eaten nothing for hours, Rufus was a little weak in the knees himself, but what maniac would risk his life for breakfast? "Are you going up there?" he asked, trying to look invisible.

"I go where I please," she replied. "After all, I am a cat."

Moments later, the friends polished off a sea trout, admiring the skeleton as if it were an art exhibit. "The barbarian spoke to me," Asha teased. Rufus looked up.

44

"The dog? He probably said he'd been planning to eat you—
then remembered you're a cat."

"I see living with humans hasn't curbed your sense of humor,"
Asha observed. "Pretty sure he asked how fast you could run."
Turning for the trees, she added, "Don't look now, but the devil
beast is tracking us. Fortunately, I know a shortcut."

Rufus felt a twinge of indigestion. It was always a mistake to
eat before taunting death. And Uncle Oscar, the old tom who'd
taught him so much when he was tiny, had repeatedly cautioned,
"Beware of shortcuts, catling. Most are anything but."

8

CHAPTER EIGHT

Undercover Brainiac

Monday marked Jack's second week in the horror show titled "Welcome to Your New School." Seven more weeks of agony till summer. School had always been a nightmare for Jack, who was obsessively, painfully shy.

"You'll grow out of it," Sam had told him. Right. He would have to be... what? Eighty? Ninety?

Who could wait? At twelve, Jack had already mastered every key to shyness survival: avoid sudden moves, make zero eye contact, slouch till they mark you absent.

These strategies were overkill in algebra. Near-sighted as a mole, Mr. Aragon only called on people in the front row. Fewer names to memorize that way.

Mrs. Higsby had taught history for as long as people had roamed the earth. Filling young minds with the wisdom gathered in that time was challenging enough without interruptions. "My dears, we'll get to questions down the road," she told the class. Jack wanted to hug her. Almost.

His luck ran out with Mr. Moody, who sought students' opinions on everything but the time of day. "I've met starfish chattier than you," he told Jack. "If you're shy, get over it." *Get over it?* That would be like getting over red hair.

The blustery science teacher, whose socks never seemed to match, didn't wait for a private moment to say this. Oh, no. He broadcast it. In stereo. The whole class dropped their pencils, waiting for the new kid to say something earth shattering. Jack wanted to melt into the floor.

When he tried inching toward the back of the room, a Moody thunderbolt nearly detonated his heart: "Plotting your escape, Jack? Let's get you UP FRONT where I can hear all those

IMPORTANT THINGS you have to say. And remember to SPEAK UP!" People like this should come with volume control.

Lexi said her maternal grandmother Ruby, a former teacher and member of the Lakota Nation, considered quiet people thinkers. Jack wished he had a grandmother like Ruby. Or someone, anyone, who suspected introverts were undercover brainiacs.

He also wished he were playing baseball. Lexi had her own mitt, and unlike Sam, could catch anything Jack threw—and feed it right back.

After school, they stood behind a chain-link fence, watching Doc, the Wildcats' ace pitcher. "Here comes a slider," Lexi whispered. One nanosecond later, the ball came sidewinding over the plate.

Lexi called every pitch, while Jack couldn't distinguish sliders from fastballs from changeups. Not that the pitchers were giving him much help. Aside from Doc, most could barely find the strike

48

zone, though Lexi said that would change soon enough. Three things mattered: speed, control, and how you held the ball as you released it. Someone named Rainy Day had taught her this.

"Keep watching, Jack," she told him. "They'll get better. And you'll catch on. You're smart."

No one had ever told Jack he was smart. He played that conversation over and over in his head.

49

CHAPTER NINE

Nothing to Get Riled Up About

Had it not been for the coyote, they might never have found the hideout.

After three days of unproductive hunting, the lanky predator was surviving on swamp grass. He would have preferred a fat rabbit or even a sinewy gopher to a cat, but could no longer afford to be picky. The felines were trotting along at a pace that would make capture a breeze. The skinny black one seemed wary, but she was barely a mouthful. He could easily get the big red one, who kept pausing to sniff ferns.

Asha's shortcut led them down an abandoned trail through old growth so dense it blocked all but the merest wisp of sunlight. The grove was good news and bad for the coyote. He could fade into the dark, except for his eyes, making it easy to close in on prey. Cats

were intrepid climbers, though, and the towering trees offered myriad escape routes. He'd have to get very lucky. And very close.

They were deep into the grove, all of them, when things went haywire. Turning to look for Rufus, Asha stared into the face of a killer—poised to nab the fern sniffer in one leap.

"When I tell you," she whispered to Rufus, "scale that tree like your tail's on fire. *Now!*" Terrified, he did what she asked, reaching, digging, spiraling round the trunk, eyes wide, throat sucking in air. He had no idea how high he'd gone when he stopped to breathe. Asha was ten feet above him.

Below, dirt, sweat, and fur flew in all directions. A bundle of snarling fury had barreled into the coyote, hurling him skyward. The fiend nipped at the coyote's haunches, neck, feet, tail, seemingly everywhere at once. With agility a contortionist would have envied, the scraggly hunter wrenched himself free from this lunatic dervish, and streaked for the meadow, eyes rolled back, ears flat to his head.

Asha and Rufus stared down at Mac, now gazing up calmly, as if ravenous coyotes were nothing to get riled up about. Which for him, they weren't.

"You need to see this," Asha was saying. Who was she talking to? *Rufus?* Was she *daft?*

Rufus felt his heart was not up to any more surprises. He'd already been hypnotized—and nearly eaten alive. Then, while being rescued by a dog of all things, he'd stormed up a tree that reached into the cosmos, moving three times faster than normal cats were meant to move. He ached all over. His fur was a mess. He wished profoundly that he were home by the woodstove, enjoying crab cakes, grilled trout—or anything, really—basking in the sweet scents of civilization. But he wasn't. So, thinking this was as good a day to die as any, Rufus headed higher, noting that for the moment, he couldn't see Asha at all.

10

A Matter of Opinion

Ancient, gnarly, the mother tree in which they found themselves had begun life as a tenacious seedling some five hundred years back, surviving droughts that withered all but the most resilient, and storms fierce enough to drive many a tree to ground. Her neverending network of moisture-seeking roots had pulled water from unimaginable distances, sustaining the tree and the numerous relatives and offspring surrounding her. Countless porcupines, squirrels, and raccoons had nested in her arms, along with swarms of spiders and insects, throngs of birds, and virtual acres of moss and lichen.

This was a tree that could make her own earth, her own weather, shedding foliage that slowly dissolved into rich loam, capturing clouds whose rain flowed in bountiful rivulets to a

thirsty earth below, releasing oxygen that enabled forest dwellers to breathe.

Twenty-some feet up, where the tree had been struck twice by lightning, new growth had forked into smaller shafts, forming an inverse tripod. There, on some long-ago date, someone had placed a row of heavy planks, bolted together and sawed to hug the tree's rounded trunks. Time had weathered the planks to an oyster shell gray, mossy fingers caressing their silky surface.

Tracing the perimeter, Asha picked up the lingering scent of crows, who no doubt considered the tree theirs. That would be just like crows. Rufus, who avoided edges whenever possible, plunked down in the middle, grateful for the chance to make himself into a cat again.

Asha gazed over the crystal-dappled inlet, through the sun-speckled canopy abuzz with its chirruping riot of squirrels and rush of warblers, and across the creek-etched wetlands. What a perfect lookout. Rufus, meanwhile, heard twigs snapping, feet scurrying, something gibbering. *What was out there?*

"Coyotes don't climb trees," Asha assured him. "Eagles can't see us. It's the safest place you could be."

That's a matter of opinion, Rufus thought. "We'll waste away eating lichen."

"Hunger keeps us alert," Asha said. "The fisherman will share tomorrow. And if he doesn't, crabs are easy prey."

Raw crabs. For breakfast. This life of terror and deprivation wasn't winning Rufus over. "It could thunder," he said. Rufus hated thunder. Any weather, in fact, offered a good excuse for heading in.

Asha sniffed the air. "That storm's far off. Lightning would be impressive from here, though."

Till it kills you, Rufus thought. This wasn't going at all well. "Come home with me," he pleaded.

Asha was silent for a moment. "I am home. With nothing between me and the stars."

Rufus liked things, *oodles* of things, between him and the stars. "You could die out here," he said.

56

"If I'm lucky, yes," Asha replied, her eyes softening as she looked at Rufus. "You have many friends. I have one. That makes your every visit a gift. But eventually, we both know you'll return to the humans. I cannot. Freedom for safety will always be, for me, a bad trade."

CHAPTER ELEVEN

Finding Waihona

Lexi's Hawaiian father, an ecological researcher, was "off somewhere saving reefs." Lexi had been ten when she'd lost her mother. "Indigo believed trees had healing power," Lexi told Jack, meandering farther, then farther still, from any visible trail. The forest closed behind them as they wandered deep into the darkness of the old growth.

"She said every living thing had a soul," Lexi went on, "and it was her job as an artist to bring that out. Ruby's always telling stories about her. She says no one's ever gone while they're alive in someone's story." *A comforting way to think about death*, Jack decided. *If you had to think about it at all.*

Just when the forest had absorbed the last drop of light, they emerged into a clearing, where blinding sun spilled over a primordial tree. They paused, transfixed.

"I think we've stepped into a fable," Jack said. Before them was… what? *A tiny door?* "Who lives here? A miniature wizard?"

They eased the door open. Cautiously. Eight black eyes stared out from one decidedly hairy face. Jack closed the door and backed away. "Who was that?"

Lexi laughed. "The wizard, I presume. Disguised as a jumping spider. *Shhh.* They have remarkable hearing. And vision—thanks to those multiple eyes. They're acrobats too, swooping from draglines to capture prey."

Jack looked up, hoping the wizard didn't have an oversized cousin hanging about. That's when he saw… *something.* Lexi smiled. "This tree knows we're here," she said softly. "Feel it beckoning us? We mustn't say no."

Lichen-covered spurs formed a rustic ladder of sorts. Helpful to those who weren't cats. They climbed into the clouds. Fog rolled away like a cape, and a roofless treehouse appeared. "Whoever built this meant it to stay hidden," Lexi whispered. "It feels like someone's sanctuary."

60

They named the hidden fort Waihona. Hawaiian for a place to keep treasures. Not gold. But a rug Lexi's grandmother had made when she was fourteen. And books. Dozens of them... *The House on Mango Street*, *Hatchet*, *The Trouble with Poetry*, *The Hobbit*, *The Book Thief*, *Two Old Women*, *Harbor Me*, *The Soul of an Octopus*, *To Kill a Mockingbird*... Reading, Jack discovered, was a whole new experience when you chose the books yourself.

"You hitch a ride through another reality," Lexi said, "and come back changed. In Hawaiian culture, we believe most things of value cannot be held in our hands. But books are different. They contain worlds."

Waihona became a place to talk of things they discussed nowhere else: what it means to be someone's friend, whether God hears us, what to choose if you could be a genius at one thing, how angry you could be when the universe stole someone you loved, ways of knowing what is true... and whether finding Waihona had been an accident.

62

"Not a chance," Lexi insisted. "We could have gone a thousand different ways through these unmapped woods. We didn't accidentally end up here. No. This tree was calling us to her."

I was mostly following you, Jack thought. But of course, that wasn't exactly accidental either.

One day, Jack noticed a carved message so close to the edge that one massive trunk had nearly enveloped it. The words spelled out *Audentes fortuna iuvat*, followed by the letters R. J. & "T. T. R."

"R. J.? Those are Mr. Peabody's initials," Lexi noted. She peered down the mammoth trunk. "I can't quite picture the poet climbing up here—but imagine writing with a mystical tree whispering in your ear."

Why were the letters T. T. R. in quotation marks? And what did *Audentes fortuna iuvat* mean? They vowed to keep Waihona and its little wizard their secret. Two others, of course, had already staked their claim. They didn't read Latin either. But they did appreciate the rug.

63

12

CHAPTER TWELVE

We All Have Magic in Us

Asha heard them coming, and peered down. *Snails climb faster than humans,* she thought. Luckily, these two weren't being chased by coyotes. The small one pulled herself up, coming face to face with Rufus. "Hello, there! Does the wizard know you've moved in?"

Jack, right behind her, said, "This is that red cat I told you about. The one that reads minds."

From the shadows, knowing blue eyes looked out. *Ah, the Queen of Cats,* Lexi thought. *Those eyes miss nothing.*

Not even a wizard dangling from a gossamer thread high above them. Asha doubted the humans had noticed him yet—humans weren't big noticers. Although, that tiny one was...*eerily catlike.*

Rufus, more interested in food than in nimble wizards, watched the boy pull something from his backpack. Nothing edible, but the next best thing. A book. He curled up on Jack's lap, following the turning pages as if Tolkien were speaking right to him. Which is how authors want all readers to feel.

Later, as they headed home, Jack said, "That red cat has magic in him."

"We all have magic in us," Lexi replied.

"Not Mr. Moody," Jack said, pitching a pine cone into a tall tree— and unleashing a torrent of protests from one very miffed squirrel. "That guy lives to torture me with his hundred-decibel voice."

"A big voice can mask a lot of fear," Lexi said.

Jack scoffed. "The only thing that'll take Hurricane Moody down is laryngitis."

"Or fear of never being the teacher he wants to be. You keep him going, you know. While no one else is listening, you sit there with *Tell Me More!* tattooed on your forehead."

65

If this is true, Jack thought, *would it kill the guy to be nicer to the one person who made him believe he could teach?*

"He sees brilliance lurking under that cloak of shyness, Jack. He's dying for you to let it out. The longer you stay silent, the louder he's going to get."

Jack couldn't sleep that night.

A New Pitcher

As Mr. Moody rhapsodized over monarchs, Jack's mind drifted. Mrs. Peabody was helping the class plant a butterfly garden and seemed to know every plant essential to monarch happiness. She'd told Jack she had a cat named Rufus, who attracted butterflies like some furry milkweed.

Jack couldn't bear to tell her that no butterfly whispering feline could rival that red forest cat.

"Who knows what the word *riparian* means?" Mr. Moody was asking. "Anyone?"

Lexi looked at Jack. *Answer.* And he came oh so close. But at the last minute he pretended, like everyone else, to be engrossed in his doodling. The moment passed, and Mr. Moody explained that *riparian* referred to the area along a river or other body of water. Jack bit his lip.

"This is crazy," he mumbled, louder than he'd intended. Mr. Moody asked if he had something to share. *YES! FEAR IS GNAWING ON MY BRAIN!* he screamed. Silently.

"Before you go, everyone," the teacher said, raising his voice over the din of shuffling papers, "Coach Ramirez wants a word. I need your attention for *FIVE MORE MINUTES.*"

The baseball coach was young—and nervous. Fans were counting on him to turn the Wildcats' so-so season around, but his best shot at making that happen was packing for California.

"Hi, everybody," he began, and Mr. Moody asked if he could please speak up. Jack stifled a laugh.

"Uh, certainly," Coach Ramirez continued. "Sad to report, we've lost Doc. Well, we didn't *lose* him. He's moving." The coach chuckled, but students either didn't get the joke or weren't paying attention.

"Anyway. I'm here to recruit a new pitcher." He smiled at the students, none of whom smiled back because they were all staring at the clock. "Who wants to take our Wildcats to a championship?"

One hand went up.

14

CHAPTER FOURTEEN

The Good Guy Test

Jack was moseying toward the inlet, tossing a baseball, when a whirring sound drew his eyes to the dock. The fisherman was casting, putting that fly right where he wanted it to go. It was a little like pitching, Jack thought. This guy sure had the eye—and the arm—for it.

Unfortunately, meeting new people was about Jack's least favorite thing. He could hear the fisherman giving him the standard greeting: "What grade are you in? Do you like school?" And the ever popular "Wow, that's some red hair you've got there!" There was no good response to that.

Maybe he should turn around. Oh, boy. Too late. The fisherman's dog was heading right for him. Next thing Jack knew, Mac was sniffing his pockets, working his muzzle under

Jack's hand. Animals were the best, Jack thought. They didn't ask questions with answers they didn't care about anyway, or make stupid comments about your hair.

The fisherman detached a fly as Jack approached. "Hi, there," he said. "Lookin' for somebody?"

"I was wondering if you'd seen Lexi," Jack said. *Did the fisherman even know her?*

"You must be one of the good guys," Rainy replied, grinning. "You're friends with Lexi, and this fellow has obviously taken a shine to you. So, you passed the good guy test with two of my favorite people."

A dog wasn't exactly a person, but Jack liked thinking of him that way, and liked it that the fisherman did, too. Impulsively, Jack did something he'd never done—reached out his hand. "I'm Jack," he said.

"Rainy Day Doolittle. Call me Rainy. Your other new friend here is Mac." Mac wagged his tail on cue. *So, this was the guy who'd taught Lexi about pitching.*

"Mind if I ask where you're headed with a baseball mitt?" Rainy asked. Jack said he'd surprised himself by volunteering to be the Wildcats' new pitcher. He'd been hoping Lexi would help him practice.

"You, my friend, have just solved one of my problems," Rainy told him. "You've no idea how hard it is to find someone who can play a decent game of catch." With that, he gathered up his fishing gear and headed for home, indicating Jack should follow—which cheered Mac right down to the ground.

When they arrived, Rainy opened a shed that held, Jack thought, the most incredible stash of everything a person could ever want: fishing gear, glass floats, kayaks, knotted climbing ropes, camping supplies, a vintage guitar, and several Louisville Slugger bats.

After a bit of rummaging, Rainy retrieved a comfortably broken-in mitt and some well-used baseballs. "Used to play a little myself," he told Jack. "Let's find an open spot and throw a few. We'll

let Mac field for us." Jack wasn't sure how that would go, but Mac turned out to be a champion outfielder, snagging the few balls Jack threw wide, running them back in record time, and dropping them right at the fisherman's feet. They played until Mac was the only one who could see the ball.

In the deepening twilight, with trees silhouetted against a vermillion sky, they strolled back, laughing, punching shoulders, reliving their best throws and wildest errors. It was the longest Jack had gone without missing his dad.

One Tough Audience

Writing is easier when someone else does it," R. J. remarked the following morning, deleting another line and looking around for Rufus. The big cat was both muse and paperweight—and the poet felt lost without his cohort's inspiring presence.

"You writers spend hours pounding some raggedy phrase into submission," RuShi said, pulling something lemony from the oven, "when the surest way to a critic's heart is a fresh baked scone."

"Not if I'm the baker," R. J. told her. "A critic chips one tooth, and there goes my review. You know, this rubbish reads like someone else wrote it."

"Ah, you picked up on that," RuShi said. "Guess my improvements gave me away."

"Since you're on a roll, sneak in later and tweak this latest drivel," R.J. said. "My brain needs a break."

Minutes later, they were at the inlet, buying fish. "We came for two reasons," the poet told Rainy. "This lovely lady keeps losing her cat, which is hard to explain given how big he is. And how slowly he runs."

"Only cat I know lives under the dock," Rainy said. "And she ain't slow. Got rid of a wily old thief that was pilfering my fish. A rat," he added, seeing their startled looks.

"Here's the best part," he went on. "She saunters up to Mac every morning like they're best mates meeting for coffee. Not one cat in a thousand has that kind of sand."

So, this was where Asha had taken up residence. Would Rufus stray this far? Even for Asha?

The one in a thousand cat and her slow-running friend were, in fact, watching this whole scene from Waihona, where Rufus

was recounting sea stories. Since feral cats routinely court death, entertaining them is no job for the squeamish—or unimaginative. Rufus was giving it all he had.

"Tell the one about Millie," Asha urged, stretching out on the rug.

Millie had been an octopus of wicked intelligence—which, as anyone who's known an octopus can testify, is no small thing. She'd hung around a fishing trawler in the South Pacific, and according to Uncle Oscar, who'd lived in the wheelhouse, came aboard nightly to partake of the day's catch.

"You mean to tell me octopuses can crawl out of the sea?" Asha asked, as if hearing this story for the first time.

Rufus leaned in. "Picture this. Eight. Sucker. Covered. Arms. Powerful enough to take an octopus anywhere she chose to go—or drag you to your doom. Plus, three beating hearts. And blood bluer than the sky."

"Sounds like you're making things up," Asha said, knowing he wasn't. "What color was she?"

"Whatever worked in the moment," said Rufus. "Red as coral when she got excited, green as kelp—or so brown and pebbly that wretches on the ocean floor would never see her coming."

"If I could pull off a stunt like that," Asha said, "think how dangerous I'd be." She sat up. Rufus was coming to the good part.

"One night, Millie climbed aboard, cracked the fish trap like some tattered clam shell, and hauled the petrified crab to starboard. Oscar leaped from the bridge, latching onto that crab like she was his long-lost mother. Millie wrestled them both into deep before the fishermen could spit."

"Well?" Asha prompted. "Don't stop now."

"Uncle Oscar surfaced on port side, that giant crab in his mouth, pincers snapping like evil tongs. And no Millie. The sailors pulled the water-logged castaways from the brine, and cooked up a

crab jamboree. From that night on, Oscar had all the fish he could eat. Plus a cushy bed in the captain's quarters."

"Tell it again," Asha said, flopping back onto the rug. "You skipped the whole underwater battle."

Rufus sighed. Feral cats. One tough audience.

80

16

The Winning Ticket

As Jack entered the classroom, Lexi slipped him a note. *Fortune favors the brave. What… ??*

"Who remembers how far monarch butterflies migrate?" Mr. Moody asked hopefully. They'd just discussed this—yet students' wild guesses showed no one had been listening.

Twenty miles!

With those giant wings? Fifty miles! No, wait—a hundred!!

Mr. Moody looked like a man with a losing lottery ticket. Whatever the secret to great teaching might be, it had eluded him. As he began daydreaming about a job in sales, Jack's hand went up.

"Monarchs fly up to three thousand miles," Jack said—and the class exploded with laughter. Students held their sides.

Three thousand miles?? News flash! That's impossible!

They're butterflies, man, not jets!

If classrooms had trap doors like theaters, Jack thought, he'd pull the lever right now.

"Settle down, everyone," Mr. Moody was saying. "Jack's right, actually. Monarchs might look frail, but they're secret athletes." The laughter subsided, and Mr. Moody sensed an opportunity.

"Do you recall where western monarchs start their journey, Jack? Or where they wind up?"

Eyes pinned Jack like an insect to a board. *Take a breath... They can't eat you alive.*

"They fly from the northern U.S. or Canada to California. Sometimes Mexico."

"Exactly right," Mr. Moody declared, shredding a monster wave of confidence. "It can take several generations to go north, but the superheroes fly south in one astonishing trip. You might say they're the jets of the insect world." He shot a meaningful look at the wisecracking student.

"How can a butterfly travel so far," Mr. Moody pressed on, "without getting lost?"

The class turned to the resident scientist.

"Monarchs have a brain the size of a sesame seed," Jack said, "but they use their antennae like a compass."

The room went silent.

Mr. Moody was beaming. Finally. He held the winning ticket. Someone else was smiling with her eyes. And nobody with a brain bigger than a sesame seed was laughing anymore.

84

You Don't Have to Be Babe Ruth

A blood-orange sun nestled into its lavender cloud hammock as people crammed the stands for the big game. Which Jack wished they'd stop referring to as the BIG GAME. They couldn't help it. The Wildcats needed two more wins before regionals, and tonight faced the undefeated Hawks, best team in the league. This would be a nail biter.

"Trust your arm," Lexi told him. "If you can nick a mile-high branch with a wimpy pine cone, you can sure as heck hit a big fat catcher's mitt with a baseball. Remember our motto—*Audentes fortuna iuvat.*"

"*Fortune favors the brave,*" they recited together. Who could forget? Lexi quoted it daily.

As Jack entered the dugout, Coach Ramirez was revving up the team. "Rip, you're the fastest shortstop the world's ever seen. Snap those grounders to Newsie on first—and News, you be ready." Jack recalled The Ripster letting many a grounder and fly ball slip through his mitt, but maybe believing you were the fastest shortstop the world had ever seen could improve your game.

"Swing at anything that invades your strike zone," the coach went on. "You don't have to be Babe Ruth. Just get on base. And Jack—knock 'em dead, kid!"

Nerves got to Jack in the first inning, and he threw more balls than strikes. Worse, it didn't seem to matter what he pitched. The Hawks sent everything but dirt balls into orbit.

In the second inning, Jack hit his stride, getting three players out after one scored run. The Wildcats came to life too, with five hits. Three runners made it home, for a score of 4-3, Hawks.

Then—things surged into overdrive. Strikeouts piled up. Jack hijacked every ground ball that tried to skirt by him, firing them

86

to Newsie on first, K.C. on second, Diego on third. In the fourth
and fifth innings, he seized lightning bolts launched by two of the
Hawks' best hitters. Both were dumbfounded when Jack ruined
their plans to even make first.

Despite Jack's heroic efforts though, by the bottom of the
sixth, the score was 8-3 Hawks. And Jack was up to bat. With bases
loaded and two outs, he stood an astronomically good chance of
leading his team into utter annihilation.

Backing away from the plate to adjust his helmet, Jack glanced
at the stands, and someone familiar stared back. From inside a
backpack. Was it… the mind reading cat from the forest? Was *that*
Mrs. Peabody's butterfly-magnet-Rufus? Jack's mouth fell open.

"Still thinking of batting tonight, son?" the umpire asked—
and Jack felt a chill as he stepped to the plate. He risked a last look,
and it cost him. "Strike ONE!" No one had to tell the umpire to
SPEAK UP.

The second pitch came in well below his knees. He swung anyway. "Strike TWO!"

Frustrated, Jack took a no-holds-barred swing at the third pitch—and connected. The loud crack sounded right. Felt right. A high, long flyer sailed over the infield, over the outfield, and deep into "Nowhereville" beyond the back fence. Jack watched in disbelief. Then someone yelled, "Jack! Run!" He came to. And ran. Channeling Rickey Henderson. Billy Hamilton. Secretariat. People sprang to their feet, stomping, cheering, screaming his name. Only one fan was quiet. Guiding Jack home with those green eyes.

No one else scored that night. It didn't matter. The Wildcats may as well have crushed the World Series.

Following the obligatory high fives, Lexi showered confetti over the whole team. The Hawks stood around with blank faces, speechless. Did the Wildcats think they'd won? No one paid the visitors any mind.

88

RuShi was swinging her imaginary bat for all she was worth, the poet nodding, curving an arm to mirror the ball's trajectory. Rufus turned toward Jack with a look that said, "Way to rock it, pitcher man."

90

18

A Real Gene Kelly Moment

It would be a night to remember. Rainy built a campfire to celebrate the Wildcats' "Near Victory," pulled his Martin guitar from the wall, and began taking requests.

Birds hushed their avian chit-chat. Waves stilled one another along the shore. Stars came out in droves to join the festivities, and the wind held its breath, listening as fans in high spirits sang every folk and pop song they knew—and quite a few they didn't. As they thundered through "This Land Is Your Land," someone interrupted.

"I can't take it anymore!" It was the history teacher. *Were we that bad?* Jack wondered, as Mr. Moody steered him away from the crowd. But it wasn't about the singing.

"Florence—uh, Mrs. Higsby—resigns every year," the teacher explained. "It's sort of a tradition. She'll recant in a minute.

Though maybe she shouldn't this time. You may have noticed she tires easily, even if her mind's still bright as the North Star." Mr. Moody, who clearly had something more on his mind, smiled at the pitcher.

"You were pure poetry on that mound, Jack," he said. "Maybe bring your mitt to class." The teacher started back—then had a new thought. "Of course," he added, "the power's not in the mitt. You can be fearless, apparently, when you need to be."

Fearless. Some response was clearly called for here. "*Audentes fortuna iuvat!*" was on the tip of Jack's tongue, but quoting Latin is risky business unless you're looking to show off. Thankfully, the crowd came to his rescue.

These feet have minds of their own!

Hope nobody's filming this!!

As predicted, Mrs. Higsby had withdrawn her resignation, and Lexi had suggested celebrating with a circle dance. Already, folks had racked up more toe injuries than giraffes in spike heels.

"Listen, everyone—let's straighten out this dance troupe before we kill ourselves!" Mr. Moody said in his most teacherly voice. "Follow me!"

Mr. Moody had never led a dance of any kind, but he'd led plenty of other things. What could be so different?

Rainy watched the company whoop and holler their way toward the dock, dimly lit only by fishing lanterns. "Careful!" he called out. "That water's fifteen feet deep—and cold!"

No one heard him. Certainly not Mr. Moody, who was nearing the end of the L's short arm, and probably had some notion of pivoting at that point, directing the ensemble back to the campfire. He hadn't counted on the domino effect of all those bodies shipwrecking his pirouette.

It was a real Gene Kelly moment until his right foot missed the dock entirely. He was still spinning when he hit the water.

19

CHAPTER NINETEEN

Small Price to Pay

Those close to the splash laughed at first—then froze as a ghostly face broke the surface. "I can't swim!" the teacher gasped. Before the bay swallowed him.

If there'd ever been a time for fortune to favor the brave, this was it. Only Jack's legs wouldn't move. *Was he dreaming?* It was Sam. She'd become a human anchor, securing him in place.

People would later recall a shadowy form ripping along the dock, cleaving the water like a missile. As Mr. Moody sank into the cold for a third time, Mac came up under one arm. The teacher seized the big dog in a death grip that would have taken most swimmers down. Unruffled, Mac propelled the wheezing aquanaut to shore as if he were weightless.

Mr. Moody had lost both shoes, but they'd hurt like blistering blazes, so good riddance. He was more concerned about his glasses. Without them, he could barely make out who anyone was.

"That was… my first time… in the ocean," he coughed out, suggesting this routine would improve with practice.

Numerous hugs squeezed all remaining oxygen out of the teacher. Small price to pay for a man who couldn't recall being hugged. Ever. "Thank goodness you're alive," someone said. A sentiment Mr. Moody hadn't expected to hear from anyone. Even family.

Folks shoved the teacher into Rainy's giant boots and hooded slicker—more of a nuisance than a help to a person already drenched. Mr. Moody was soon steaming like a clam.

"Let's get this good man home," Rainy said. Eager to make up for their earlier failure as lifeguards, people whipped out flashlights and began gamely ad-libbing "Octopus's Garden"—which Mr. Moody had requested. Supposedly. Since he could

barely be heard from inside the cavernous hood, it's hard to say what he requested.

They arrived to find the teacher's front door unlocked, the house cave-like. No one volunteered to go in. That is, almost no one.

Rufus leaped from RuShi's backpack and marched into the dark as if summoned by the Queen. RuShi called to him, but cats are superbly gifted at ignoring that sort of thing. The poet squeezed her hand. "The man could use some company," he said. "And who better?"

Mr. Moody's first impulse was to scoop the cat up, but scooping cats is tricky under the best of circumstances, and all but impossible when trapped in a giant slicker. "There must be some mistake," he called out from the hood. "Cats don't even like me."

The poet stepped forward. "This isn't your usual cat," he told the slicker. "Converting skeptics into cat lovers is his hobby. He's helping revise a poem, though, so we need him home by breakfast."

Breakfast? Surely, RuShi thought, the red cat would return before that. He might well have—had he not become sublimely preoccupied.

20

CHAPTER TWENTY

Cat Lover?

Once inside, Mr. Moody struggled out of the hot, rubbery paraphernalia. *Cat lover?* Ha! That would be the day. But—he was alive. He could put up with a cat, he supposed. For one night.

My word, he had the munchies. All that dancing. To say nothing of his unintended dip in the water. He rounded up some cookies and milk. Hold on, though. Cats didn't eat cookies, and he didn't want to be a poor host, cat lover or not. Would leftover salmon do?

Mr. Moody headed for the bedroom, juggling plates. Something was rising from the bed, moving his way. He fumbled for his spare glasses, the ones with over-sized lenses. Ah, it was only the cat. Heavens, he was big. And did cats generally make themselves at home like this?

The pungent scent of salmon had Rufus dizzy with anticipation. A human who enjoyed snacks in bed? Beyond civilized. Not
to mention, the décor in this room was... in a word, eye-popping.

A reef aquarium filled the far wall. Bubbles erupted as fish
vanished and reappeared through seagrass and coral. It was hard
to look away, even to eat. Rufus had seen fish in the bay, but they
didn't come in this kaleidoscope of colors. Plus, you had to watch
them from above. This was infinitely better—like being in the
water, only with none of the mess and bother.

"The clownfish are my favorites," Mr. Moody said, amazed by
how natural it felt talking to a cat. It felt natural to Rufus as well,
of course. Humans always spoke to him. He couldn't help noticing
that Mr. Moody looked rather fish-like himself, his eyes large and
luminous behind those gigantic lenses. Humans put the strangest
things on their heads.

"It was a good day," Mr. Moody went on. "Funny thing to say
on a day you nearly drown. Though I don't suppose you'd know

99

anything about that." Actually, Rufus knew all about it, having been through a similar experience involving disgruntled geese. He began purring in a manner the teacher found soothing.

"I found out tonight I have friends," Mr. Moody continued, removing the glasses to wipe his eyes. "One was a dog." He put his glasses back on. Through the lenses, the cat's green eyes looked astoundingly wise. This was clearly a being one could trust. Even confide in. "Something came to me. Oddly enough, while thrashing about in the bay."

Rufus would have been the first to admit that time underwater could dramatically reset one's priorities. He sensed the teacher was coming to the point, and took care not to interrupt.

"I've spent years ferreting out students' weaknesses instead of helping them discover their strengths. That young pitcher's a different person tonight—and I did that. Can you believe it?" Rufus himself had a knack for bolstering self-esteem. But this was hardly the time to dredge up all that.

Mr. Moody nodded at the aquarium. "Watch that angelfish," he said. Rufus had already noticed a striped troublemaker gliding with diabolical intentions toward a small blue fellow. Humans loved pointing out things they thought cats had missed. Rufus didn't mind playing along. This wasn't the first time it had occurred to him how little it took to make a human happy.

21

CHAPTER TWENTY-ONE

Exceedingly Good Friends

Mr. Moody had forgotten to close the kitchen window. And so, the following morning, his night visitor leaped out as one curious blue jay hopped in. *Just in time*, Rufus thought. He'd felt a bit guilty leaving this fragile human alone. He'd be fine now, with someone to talk to.

Normally, nothing called to Rufus like home, hearth, and breakfast. But today, eager to tell Asha about fish swimming on walls, he headed for the inlet, arriving just as Razi poked his head out of the tunnel. "What a night," Razi sputtered. "The humans wore out the floor fretting over you."

"Lucky you were there," Rufus said, looking round for Asha. "Cats have a genius for tamping down hysteria."

"Some do. Others have a different effect," Razi said, looking toward the inlet where The Scout, a small red fishing boat, was transporting a notorious feline firebrand to sea.

Rufus's heart clenched—even as a keening howl reverberated over the water. It was the big dog, who'd also been watching The Scout, no doubt wishing stowaways could be retrieved from the bay as handily as drowning teachers. Rufus wished the same. How quickly the world could tilt.

The Scout gained speed as it left the cove for choppier waters. Rufus had barely reunited with Asha. Now, she was bound somewhere he could not follow, no matter how brave he might talk himself into being. Did the fishermen know she was on board? What if she fell in? *Or they threw her in?*

"Humans will make a worrier of you yet," Razi said, sensing his friend's anxiety. "She won't fall—she's topped cliffs that would give you vertigo. In ice storms." Rufus recalled Asha rocketing into

the treetops, outmaneuvering that coyote. Her quick thinking had saved his life that day. Could she swim, though? How far?

"She's been on fishing boats before," Razi added. "What's to like? I don't get the allure."

It's not the boat, Rufus thought, wishing he'd kept a few nitty-gritties of that octopus story to himself.

Asha was watching them, ascending the mast as if she'd lived her whole life on The Scout. Seagulls dipped and shrieked, cheering her on. Cats consider waving undignified. So, as the boat melded into a blue-on-blue horizon, Asha said goodbye with a look that would haunt Rufus.

"How will a cat born of the wild amuse herself in that cramped space?" Razi wondered.

"Oh, she'll keep busy enough," Rufus sighed. "Guarding the catch from eight-armed bandits."

Razi's eyes narrowed. "Eight-armed bandits? You storytellers come up with some outlandish hooey."

"We're not to blame," Rufus said. "It's life. That's where stories come from."

Razi scanned the sea. "Life's a tad wackier for some than for others, I'd say. But eventually, like old Uncle Whatshisname, our thrill seeker will need an audience for those bone chilling tales she's out concocting." He turned to Rufus. "That will bring her back, you know. The chance to scare us sleepless."

A seed of hope took root in Rufus's heart. He could hear Uncle Oscar whispering, "Hang onto this one, catling. Philosophers make exceedingly good friends, 'specially on a wintry night."

CHAPTER TWENTY-TWO

Wherever You Go

Jack had no idea that a book found that spring would become a cherished possession decades later. No one imagines such things at age twelve.

The book was wrapped in a feed sack, tucked into the Wizard of Waihona's tiny hollow. They almost didn't find it. When they did, all they cared about was the bookmark: a newspaper clipping telling of a long-ago regional championship, with glowing words about the high school's "world-class pitcher," one Robert Jake Doolittle, and "the greatest young catcher ever to grace a ballfield," Johnny "Mac" McCoy. "Rainy's initials…" Lexi didn't need to finish the thought. Ruby would know.

Minutes later, Lexi's grandmother met them at the door. "Finally," she said, "I get to congratulate the pitcher who took down the invincible Hawks."

The Wildcats had won the final two games of the pre-championship series, one a shutout, the other a fight to the last pitch. Jack had caught a fly ball from outer space at the bottom of the seventh, quashing the Hawks' last shot at regionals.

"Uh, speaking of baseball..." Lexi handed Ruby the clipping.

"Where'd you find this?" Ruby asked. Gracefully ignoring the question, Lexi asked if her grandmother knew anything about Rainy, aka Robert, building a tree fort. Ruby smiled the way people do when watching someone unravel a secret, then turned to Jack.

"I see you're one of us," she said. *What did she mean?* "Been shy my whole life. Nahele—Lexi's grandfather—used to tell me, *Pretend you're brave.* No one will know the difference."

Ruby laughed. "I've seen it happen with you on that mound. Buddy, when you let the real Jack come out and play, we'd follow you to the ends of the earth.

"Shy people are just heroes in hiding, you know," she added. "We always come out if there's a reason."

Later that day, Lexi and Jack walked together to Waihona, Jack tossing a baseball while imagining a summer of reading in the trees. Then reality stepped on his toes.

"After regionals, I'm meeting my father in Hawaii," Lexi said. "To photograph reefs. It's my dream, only... I'll be gone till September."

This isn't happening, Jack thought. "You're going... across the ocean?" *Brilliant, Sherlock.*

"Gotta go where the reefs are." Lexi smiled. "I'll miss our little wizard." *And you.* She slipped the old book into his backpack. "Take care of Waihona."

Waihona for me goes wherever you go, Jack thought. He wasn't brave enough to say that, however. So, he said nothing. But eyes always reveal the truth.

Lexi lifted the shark tooth from her neck and hung it round his. "Never take this off. It'll bring you luck. And remind you of me."

Take it off? He'd die first. But—who needed a reminder? Lexi was about as forgettable as breathing. He tucked her one-of-a-kind smile into his heart.

Epilogue

It was the eve of the first regionals game. Children with flashlights combed "Nowhereville," looking for a missing baseball a young pitcher had slammed into history. They couldn't find it. No one ever would.

Asha drifted miles from land, nothing between her and the stars. Though the fishermen had invited her inside, she preferred her own digs—a healthy coil of three-quarter inch rope snugged against the wheelhouse. The full moon cast pearlescent light across a seascape so vast it stretched into eternity. Below its deceptively serene surface, the ocean churned with life, moonlight enticing the octopuses out to hunt. They were curious creatures. Asha was counting on that.

From atop a granite boulder in the poet's back yard, Rufus watched the great forever unspool, Asha's voice in his head—where he'd keep it till she returned. "Go in, Mender of Hearts," she was saying, using her old nickname for Rufus, "The universe won't go anywhere. Your humans miss you."

While the average feline found humans' fear of being alone baffling, their insatiable desire for attention suffocating, the red cat was different. Being needed fueled his soul. Increasingly, he relished his capacity to make humans believe they could do remarkable things. Heroic, impossible things.

With Rufus nearby, the poet's mind burned with an electric fever, his pen dancing over the pages. The gardener coaxed life from dusty earth, her songs of rivers and rainbows arousing forgotten longings in the stoniest hearts. A lonely teacher dared to make friends—and be one. And the young human who'd lit a whole crowd on fire? Whatever Rufus had awakened in that boy would never sleep again.

To many this might sound like magic—and it is. Only not the sort of magic that whisks time travelers to exotic realms or turns frogs into princes. Real magic begins with love and kindness. The one potion that transforms us all into what we're meant to be.

The future all-star pitcher sat on a bleacher above a moonlit ball field, fingering the tooth of a Great White. *We always come out if there's a reason.* He had a reason, a good one. He was in the middle of a story only he could write. For the reef lover and her shaman grandmother.

For Noah, the catcher who pulled shooting stars from heaven. Newsie, who guarded first base like rare earth. The Ripster, willing that hole in his glove to close. K.C., whose parents hadn't wanted her to be the only girl on the team, and who now had the best batting average in the league. And someone else.

Keep that arm in shape till I get back. The guy who'd believed from the first pitch.

115

This story began with you, Jack told the Sergeant. *You're part of it forever.*

Jack pulled the old book from his backpack, studying the title: *The Call of the Wild* by Jack London. The faded sketch bore an uncanny resemblance to an outfielder he knew.

As he flipped the cover, the inscription leaped out at him.

Dear Reader,

You didn't find this book by chance. It's been waiting for you, someone with the courage to wander and the vision to notice what others miss. Years from now, when the mother tree is a distant memory, may this book remind you that your time here was a rare and precious gift, as real as the voice of the forest that calls us all, but is heard only by a few.

~Ruby Jean and her fellow "Tree Top Reader," Nahele

THE CALL
of THE WILD
JACK LONDON

Fear and Courage

A Poem by R. J. Peabody and Rufus*

In a time so long ago
you cannot read about it,
Fear and Courage became friends.
It was Fear's idea. Courage had her doubts.

You cannot stop me from fulfilling dreams, she said.
Fear had to bite his tongue at that
touchy-feely nonsense. But—
he pretended to agree (fingers crossed).

Without mischief to make, Fear grew bored.
He chewed his fingernails. Toenails too. Nothing helped.
Creeping into his friend's thoughts,
he whispered Possibilities and Likelihoods and other Trash.

Courage told him to stifle his dang
What If's and Could Be's. Which made
Fear whine until the cows came home, and
that's not just some expression. They really showed up.

When he couldn't wipe that smile
off her magnificent face, Fear
took off to bully Uncertainty,
who couldn't decide what to do about that.

These days, Courage has countless friends.
They don't collect trophies or plaques.
Leaping tall buildings? Too flashy.
They do little things
that go unnoticed.
Unless you look.

Drop by. Hug you and mean it.
Listen. Heal loneliness with laughter.
Believe in today. Toast tomorrow.
Plant things. Write notes. Bake.
Share songs that stir the soul.
And stories that speak truth.

Courage shows up unexpectedly,
often after dark.
She is especially fond of children
and all who think the sunset
is their only friend.

119

Needless to say, she's a fan of dogs.
And certain cats.
In her spare time, she watches baseball,
cheering for both sides. Because
it's playing that takes grit.

Fear left his favorite saying on her wall:
I DARE YOU.
Be careful
what you wish for,
Courage says. Living is the
double dog dare
of all time.

Fear litters idle minds
with Regrets, and Doubts, and Tough Choices.
Pay no attention, Courage says.
Hang in and trust your heart.
Audentes fortuna iuvat.

*With significant input from RuShi,
an editor with impeccable finesse.

VANHOE
POPE'S
POEMS

Wild Places

A Poem by Lexi Kalama and and the Queen of Cats*

It's a race to the finish: The Wild versus Civilization.

The Wild was winning. At first.

What was infinite as the wilderness?

The prairie? The ocean?

Who could fell ALL the trees,

plow ALL the grasslands, force ALL buffalo into retreat,

melt ALL sprawling glaciers, put ALL great reefs to sleep?

Who in their right mind would invade

the mighty jungles, where winding vines and snakes

and spiders the size of fists stood guard?

Where rivers long as dreams flowed into forever?

And flora grew like imagination?

Oh, we can, the Civilized Ones said. We have a plan.

We'll tame the waters,

make green illegal,

assemble our arsenal:

Toxins. Pollution. Plastics.

And the mightiest of all weapons. Indifference.

With a will that stunned everyone,
the Wild refused to surrender.
The sun still sets. Not as bright, but it's there.
The stars come out. Though we cannot see them all.
A few whales still make their journey, singing of ancestors
who roamed oceans so big land was but a rumor.
Birds build nests designed by reptiles in transition.
Fish hide in reefs only sunlight can find,
while jellyfish pulse on.

The wild still thrives in fairy tales.
And the memories of people so old
no one trusts them to remember what was true.
Don't listen to them, the Civilized Ones whisper.
It was never like that. Not really.

The Wild lives on in the dreams of children,
who would rather not come in
when parents call. They're already home.
Though parents have forgotten how that feels.

Somewhere a tree grows to the sky.
They will come for it eventually with their chain saws,
their bulldozers, their cigarettes, and rough talk.
They must find it first, of course.

Till then, the tree grows and dares to be.
In that special way that trees know things,
it knows it is more than a tree.
It is a promise, a symbol, a legend.
A refuge. A source of life.

The Civilized Ones mock the notion
that trees feel or remember.
For trees aren't human, are they.
But, listen... hear that?
Above the whining saws...
Is it the wind? The river?
Ah, it's a tiny seedling
the Civilized Ones overlooked—
hugging the earth, listening for rain,
pointing to the light... and laughing... laughing...

*Written in a spot sacred to writers, readers, painters,
and other lovers of Wild Places.

124

Trees are sanctuaries. Whoever
knows how to speak to them,
whoever knows how to listen
to them, can learn the truth.
~ Herman Hesse

RuShi's Buttery Scones

Ingredients

- 2 ¼ cups flour
- 2 Tbsp baking powder
- ½ cup granulated sugar
- Pinch of sea salt
- 1 ½ sticks frozen butter, shredded
- 1 cup ice cold buttermilk (or cream)
- 2 Tbsp orange, almond, or vanilla flavoring
- 1 ½ cups of fun: dried cherries, dark chocolate bits, etc.

Directions

1. Preheat oven to 400°.
2. Whisk dry ingredients together in a large bowl.
3. Cut in shredded butter.
4. Add some fun—cherries, or whatever makes you smile.
5. Gradually add milk and flavoring to make a moist dough.
6. Placing dough on a floured surface, flatten to form an 8-inch round.
7. Cut into eight pieces (or six if you're hungry).
8. Place wedges on parchment covered sheet and bake for 12-15 minutes.
9. Serve with lemon curd and love.

*No teeth were chipped in the testing of this recipe.

The migration of western monarch butterflies,
featured in this story, is in crisis. If you'd like
to help, please go to xerces.org or Western
Monarch Call to Action. Thank you.

Vicki Spandel

I've loved writing all my life: as a classroom writing teacher, workshop coordinator, telecourse developer, editor, journalist—and for one beautiful period of time, scoring director for the Oregon State (and other) writing assessments.

Reading thousands of student essays and stories teaches you things you can learn no other way. While many students struggle with writing, thousands write not only competently, but brilliantly, touching our hearts and reminding us why we write. As James Baldwin once put it, "to change the world."

Most people know me as the author of numerous educational books on writing, notably *The 9 Rights of Every Writer* and *Creating Writers*. Last year, I gave in to my lifelong desire to write stories, and knew from the first line that I'd found my true love.

Stories are where the magic lies. You know this already. Think of the books that stole your heart from the time you first knew books existed. Chances are, they were books that took you to new worlds.

My first work of fiction, *No Ordinary Cat* (2020), features a highly intuitive feline named Rufus, whose insatiable appetite for adventure, along with a desire to discover his destiny, lures him into a wilderness he knows nothing about.

Finding Waihona (second book in a three-part series) shows that for Rufus—and for all of us—life is about learning what the heart treasures, then protecting it with everything in us.

This series speaks, I hope, to readers who love trekking along as extraordinary cats get themselves in and out of trouble, and to teachers, parents, and others looking for a book that begs to be read aloud. My goal always is to write books that are fun to "perform."

Writing fiction isn't altogether different from writing educational materials. With either, you need to do whatever it takes to keep readers tuned in. But fiction offers options that make it, for a writer, irresistible.

In fiction, anything can happen. And the characters you create get a vote on what that something will be. True, Rufus and Asha and their many friends might not exist without me. But they now run the show—and that's the joy of it.

Jeni Kelleher

I am a self-taught pastel artist who strives to capture the essence and soul of each subject I paint. Whether I'm painting a wild animal, pet, or child, the eyes are always center stage. They're the first thing I draw because eyes tell a story.

The cover for *Finding Waihona* was a special challenge because trees have no eyes. But notice the tiny door. With that door, and other small details, I wanted to give this tree a mystical look that captures the mood of the book.

People sometimes tell me that a painting of mine is incredibly lifelike. I'm always flattered by this. But realism isn't my goal. I want to create art that stirs emotion in people. They should be captivated by an image and develop an immediate personal connection.

Being an artist is a lifelong dream for me. I worked in the medical field for more than 20 years, 12 of them in hospice, before deciding to pursue this dream. In 2018, I took an online course from Jason Morgan, an incredible wildlife artist from Wales, UK. I knew immediately it was what I wanted to do. It's easy to pick up techniques when you're passionate about something, and soon I had my own business creating pet portraits.

Though I've never studied art formally, both my parents were gifted artists. My father, F. Eugene Smith, a well-known industrial designer, always told me I could do anything I set my mind to. It has taken endless hours of practice and great determination, but I feel my art evolving with each new piece.

Finding Waihona is the third book I've illustrated. I also did the illustrations for *No Ordinary Cat* (the first book in this series) and am beginning now on the illustrations for the third and final book. Working with Vicki is a joy. Each painting, like her stories, is an adventure.

Acknowledgements

In his incredible book *On Writing* (which never leaves my desk), author Stephen King says, "Writing is a lonely job. Having someone who believes in you makes all the difference."

The person who made all the difference on this book is Steve Peha (founder of *Platform Press* and *Singular Books*), development editor and designer for *Finding Waihona* as well as its predecessor, *No Ordinary Cat*.

Maybe, when you picture an editor, you see someone with a red pen and a vaguely disappointed expression. That's not Steve Peha. In Steve's world, development editing begins with visionary, imaginative questions like, *What would happen if you tried...?*

Steve's questions provoke creativity, uncover possibility, and unlock opportunity. Best of all, he asks the kinds of questions that make revision happen where it needs to happen: in a writer's head.

Thank you, Steve, for conversations that opened doors
and helped me understand what this book could be. You're the
champ at conferring with writers in a way that's both helpful and
enlightening. Thanks for believing in the book, working with me
every inch of the way, and "wrapping" it as the gift to readers I'd
always wanted it to be.

Thanks also to my brilliant illustrator Jeni Kelleher, who put
her magical touch on *No Ordinary Cat*, and didn't even blink when
I asked if she was up for another book—but immediately went out
and bought a billion new pencils in colors no one else had even
heard of.

Thank you, Jeni, for once again letting your heart rule your
hand, and for loving a quirky jumping spider and saucy crab just
as much as an elegant cat or beloved dog. Millie the octopus is
right out of Jules Verne.

A special mahalo to Hawaii educators Rose Yamada, Mililani
Hughes, PhD, Associate Professor Kekoa Harman (University
of Hawaii at Hilo), and to my dearest friend and soulmate Leila

Naka for their encouragement and for helping me delve into the meaning behind *waihona*. I hope my writing honors this beautiful concept for which English has no adequate equivalent.

It's only right to thank literary mentors who inspire us. My favorite children's authors include E. B. White, William Steig, Roald Dahl, Kenneth Grahame, and A. A. Milne. I admire them for many reasons. Most of all because their humor is honest but gentle, poking fun at life, not the poor souls struggling through it. They never write down to children, who are, after all, the brightest among us and deserve to be respected as such.

I'd also like to thank Stephen King for *On Writing*'s invaluable tips. The one that kept popping into my head as I wrote this book was "The adverb is not your friend," which I will one day tattoo on my wrist. I recited it aloud while sending many an adverb to perdition. I didn't get 'em all, but trust that those remaining are ~~diligently~~ earning their keep.

And finally, to my husband Jerry, whose patience passeth all understanding. My waihona is wherever you are. I'm leaving my desk soon, I promise.